FRANK AND FRIENDS

BOOK 1

The Birthday Party

4th Aug 2011
Best Wishes
Sylvian Davy
Linda Price

Old Bakehouse Publications

© Sylvian Day

First published in March 2011

All rights reserved

The right of Sylvian Day to be identified
as author of this work has been asserted by her
in accordance with the
Copyright, Designs and Patents Act, 1993.

Illustrations by Linda Price

ISBN 978-1-905967-29-2

Published in the U.K. by
Old Bakehouse Publications
Church Street,
Abertillery, Gwent NP13 1EA
Telephone: 01495 212600 Fax: 01495 216222
Email: theoldbakeprint@btconnect.com
Website: www.oldbakehouseprint.co.uk

Made and printed in the UK
by J.R. Davies (Printers) Ltd.

British Library Cataloguing in Publication Data: a catalogue
record for this book is available from the British Library.

Frank is a black labrador cross
he's big and strong, and has lots of
energy.

Frank loves the outdoors and going on
adventures with his friends, he has lots
of friends and sometimes they play
tricks on him, but he never complains.
Frank lives with his friend Cat who's
always making sure he eats plenty of
healthy food.

If you would like to write to Frank he
will always write back to you, and you
too can become one of Franks friends.

Here is his address:

"Frank"
Animal Row,
Cockles End
c/o 1 Sirhowy Cottages NP12 0HQ

*Frank hopes that you will enjoy these stories
about him and his friends, they get up to all
sorts of things.*

Written and Created

by

Sylvian Day

Illustrations

by

Linda Price

"Hello"

'Good morning Frank', said Cat
'do you know what day it is today?'.

Frank opened his eyes and said
'Yes Cat it's my birthday'.
'It will be a very special birthday
just for you', Cat replied and she
started singing Happy Birthday.

Cat's singing sounded more like
meowing, but it made Frank laugh,
and he was very happy.

Happy Birthday to you.
Happy Birthday to you.
Happy Birthday dear Frank.
Happy Birthday to you.

Frank then said to Cat, 'do you think any of my friends have remembered that it is my birthday today?'. 'Shall we wait and see', said Cat, 'and I will make you a delicious birthday tea. Now you go back to sleep for a little while as I have a few things to do'.

Cat then smiled at Frank and quietly closed his bedroom door.

Frank snuggled back down in his cosy bed and thought!! I wonder what Cat is going to make me for my birthday. I hope I get lots of surprises as it's only one day out of a whole year that you have a birthday. He then closed his eyes and went back to sleep.

Cat quickly picked up the brown envelope from the kitchen table. Inside were birthday party invitations, inviting some of Frank's friends to his birthday tea. Frank didn't know anything about it, so it would be a big surprise.

Cat hurried along the street posting all the invitations in everyones letterboxes.

She was very excited and thought, what a lovely day it was for Frank to have a birthday.

The sun was shining,
the birds were singing,
and Cat skipped and sang from house to house.

Cat then ran home as fast as she could. She had lots of things to do. She would make sandwiches and jelly and a birthday cake. Frank would like that very much.

I must hurry she thought, as Frank would be waking up soon.

As soon as Cat got home she started to make a chocolate cake, it was Frank's favourite and she would put a candle on the top for Frank to blow out and make a wish.

After his little sleep, Frank got out of bed and started to get dressed. He could smell something nice coming from the kitchen, so he called out and said, 'Cat, what are you cooking, it smells really nice'.

Cat answered and said, 'I told you Frank, I am making you a special birthday tea'. 'Oh yes', said Frank, 'I had forgotten about that. Thank you Cat'.

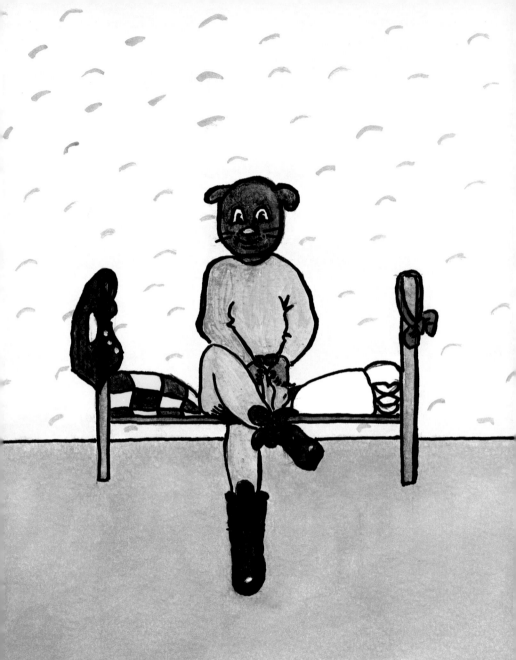

Suddenly Frank heard the
doorbell ringing
'ring ring, ring ring'.

He jumped up and hurried to
answer it. When he opened the
front door there were his friends,
Tommy Turtle, Ed the Duck,
Robbie Rabbit, Stella Hedgehog
and Molly Mole and together
they all shouted
'Happy birthday Frank'.

'Hurray', said Frank, 'I am so
happy to see you all', and he
couldn't wait to see what
presents they had brought him.

WELL come

Frank then invited everyone in. Tommy Turtle was very excited and said, 'can we give you our presents now Frank and can I give you mine first, please, please'.

Frank answered and said, 'oh yes Tommy what a good idea, I love presents'.

'Come on then Tommy let me see what you have in your parcel for me'.

Tommy then gave Frank his
present. Frank opened it up
and inside were a new pair of
gloves so he quickly tried
them on.

'Oh thank you Tommy',
said Frank 'these will keep
my paws nice and warm
and they fit perfectly'.

Ed the Duck was next and he handed Frank his present. 'Look everyone', said Frank, 'it's a new brush for my coat', and he brushed the hair on his head and laughed.

'Thank you Ed', he said, 'it is very, very nice and the bristles are nice and soft'.

Stella Hedgehog was waiting patiently to give Frank his present, as she knew he had a liking for sweet things and he would enjoy this as a treat on his birthday.

'Yummy', said Frank as he opened Stella's present, it was a big sticky lollipop.

'Now don't eat it all at once', said Stella, 'as it will give you a stomach ache'.

Robbie Rabbit then shouted, 'I'm next, I'm next'.

Robbie gave the box to Frank and he opened it up and pulled out a new blanket for his bed.

'Oh, thank you very much Robbie',
said Frank, 'this is wonderful'.

Little Molly Mole was last to give Frank his present.

Frank knew that Molly would give him something special.

Frank smiled and held up a new pair of red wellingtons. 'Happy birthday Frank', said Molly.

'Thank you Molly', said Frank, 'these are just what I needed as my other ones have holes in them'.

Frank was very happy and thought how lucky he was to have all these lovely presents.

Cat then put a party hat on everyones head and they all smiled.

Robbie Rabbit rubbed his tummy and said, 'are we going to eat now, I'm hungry'.

'Yes', said Cat, 'shall we all sit
down and have tea'.

The table was full of delicious things to eat.

There were sandwiches, lots of different cakes and biscuits, jelly and lemonade.

Tommy Turtle had to stand up on his toes as he couldn't reach the tabletop. 'Careful Tommy', said Stella 'or you will pull the tablecloth off, then your tea will be on the floor'.

Everyone laughed as he looked so funny.

Cat then shouted, 'surprise, surprise' as she came in with Frank's birthday cake with a candle on the top.

Frank was so happy and everyone started singing.

Happy Birthday to you.
Happy Birthday to you.
Happy Birthday dear Frank.
Happy Birthday to you.

With one big blow Frank blew out
the candle and made a wish.

Wishes are like secrets so he
couldn't tell anyone what he had
wished for, as if he did it wouldn't
come true.

'Hurray Hurray, Happy Birthday'
everyone called out.

Cat cut the cake and handed the first slice to Frank, she would give everyone else a slice later to take home.

'Chocolate cake', said Frank, 'my favourite. Thank you Cat'. Frank then licked his lips as he couldn't wait to eat it.

Frank enjoyed his birthday very
much and he thanked all of his
friends for making it so wonderful.
It had been a very special day.

'What a lucky dog I am', he
thought.

"Goodbye"